Don't Think and Other Stories

Femdom Mind Control

Flash Fiction – Vol. 36

S.B.

Disclaimer

This is a work of fiction. Names, characters, business, events, and incidents are the products of the author's imagination. Any resemblance to actual persons, living or dead, or actual events is purely coincidental. All characters are over 18.

Table of Contents

Let the women in your life do all the thinking for you.

Thank you to all patrons of Spell... B-O-U-N-D.

A Task a Day…

Amanda picked up the wet sponge and squeezed the tepid water over her breasts, eyes peering outside yet seeing nothing but her Mistress' face. She had cleaned every window as instructed and was finally allowed a moment of pleasure.

"A task a day keeps my conscious mind away. I will obey," she muttered. The enslaving mantra was always at the tip of her tongue, binding her to desires she never thought she would have. Foam sliding down her bare mid-drift, she picked up her smartphone and sent a picture to her owner before sitting on the cold floor, waiting for her next instructions.

The message arrived almost immediately, punctuated by two winking emojis at the beginning. Her new command was to head to the bathroom and scrub the showerhead until it was perfectly resplendent.

"When you see your blank gaze reflected on it, insert it in your pussy and leave it there until I contact you again. Are we clear, slave?"

Yes, Mistress," Amanda replied, as if she had heard her silky voice for real. "A task a day keeps my conscious mind away. I will obey."

Amanda stood up and walked mechanically to the upper floor. She didn't remember how long she had been working for, nor if she had put on any clothes after getting up from bed. Details like that were meaningless clutter in what was supposed to be a perfectly balanced and structured mind. Her purpose was clear: she lived to serve, nothing more.

An only child, Amanda discovered she was into girls at fifteen when a cousin from Europe first stole a kiss and then her heart. Getting into a relationship had never been easy for her, but the same couldn't be said about taking on the submissive role when she was in one. Thinking was hard, and she hated to call the shots in any situation unless there was no other choice. Mistress understood that, and she always followed her lead, even if she didn't understand it.

"That's what trust is," she thought like a good little brainwashed working drone.

Mistress' name was... Mistress. No other designation made her justice. The woman that owned her lived somewhere in Australia while she was stuck in Shithole, Wyoming. She often dreamed of going to her, carrying nothing but her collar and leash and throwing herself at her feet. Perhaps one day she could do that, but until then, the mantras and hypnotic triggers would have to suffice. She entered the bathroom and shivered, the weight of her suggestions reinforcing the truth of her servile condition. Real people had ideas and a will of their own. Fac-similes like her had the bliss of mindless routines. What more could she ask for?

Amanda wrapped her hands on the showerhead, the silver metal slithering between her fingers like a snake looking for a meal. She was it, ready to be devoured.

"A task a day keeps my conscious mind away. I will obey," she repeated in-between writhing orgasms on the bathroom floor. Her life was perfect.

Always Worth It

Charles clenched his teeth as he tried to break free from the thick ropes binding his chest, wrists, and ankles. They were too tight, and the friction caused red gashes to form all over his skin. His man cave, the only place in the house where he felt he could truly be himself, had turned into a living nightmare.

His girlfriend Amber stood in front of him, wearing her doctor's scrubs while playing with a syringe filled with a fluorescent green liquid that nauseated him just by looking at it. It wasn't poison, and yet it spelled death, anyway. If she got her way with it, his individuality would cease to exist.

"Please don't do this!" he exclaimed.

"I must," she replied, one eye glancing at his futile attempts to resist, and the other making sure the dosage was the correct one. "You gave me no choice."

"That's crap and you know it. You made an oath not to do any harm! How can you betray it like this?"

"The definition of 'do no harm' is flexible, dear. Let's be real here: you're not doing anything worthy of note with your mind and body, so I might as well change that."

"By turning me into your servant? How is that a good thing?"

"How is it not?", she tapped the tip of the hypodermic needle and smirked. "You'll become a useful tool, and I'll never have to worry about you going astray. All things considered, it really is the best option, and you'll blindly agree with me in no time."

"Fuck! I hate you! If I weren't restrained right now, you'd be dead already!"

"Yeah, yeah, but since you can't move at all, I've nothing to worry about, right?" She finished her preparations and circled his chair before stopping right behind him, the syringe pointing at a popping vein in his neck. "Any last words before you're reborn?"

"I hope you rot in hell, bitch!"

"That's no way to talk to the love of your life, but I forgive you this time... See you soon, slave!" She pushed the plunger of the syringe, emptying the foul content in his bloodstream. The needle burned with the contact, the flow of the drugs washing away his thoughts one by one. The cascade of oblivion spread across his brain, pushing everything away in its wake until there was only pain and all-encompassing whiteness. Charles screamed, but no one listened to his plight except her. For the first time since he had remodeled the basement, he regretted spending so much money to make it completely soundproof.

* * *

He woke up two days later, snuggled in bed, Amber wrapped around his arms. Her jet-black hair smelled of roses and her lips tasted sweet on his hairy chest. Instinctively, he touched the back of his neck, but there was nothing there.

"Good morning," she cooed. "How are you?"

"Hi," he replied. "What day is it?"

"It's Monday. You were out for a while, but don't worry. I took good care of your mind while you were gone."

"Shit, that was intense! I really believed you were going to destroy me completely."

"Wasn't that you wanted?"

"Yes, thank you."

"You're welcome. You're such a good subject I'm always happy to oblige."

"I don't remember anything that happened after the syringe scene, though."

"Not surprised," she gently caressed his sensitive nipples. "I fractionated you so many times after that your brain will need some time to recover. I'm sure everything will come back to you."

"And if it doesn't? What then?"

I'll always treasure those memories for you. Her left hand slid down his stomach until it found his tumescent cock. "It seems you have quite the swelling here, good sir. We should take care of it right away."

"My muscles are all sore... not sure I can do a thing."

"Then don't and let me be in charge once more. Doctor's orders."

"Yes, dear." He closed his eyes and drifted in the wonderful touch of her hands. Doctor by day, mind-controller by night, Amber was everything he wanted in a partner and more. Whatever he lost of himself to her hypnotic charms was always worth it.

Change of Heart

The business meeting wasn't going as expected. Ivan sat in his publisher's office, looking at the stern man's reddish face and thinking, "What the hell is wrong with him today?". Lucas Walton was usually the most laid-back person anyone could talk to, but that day he looked like a lobster burning in hot water. Not only that, but he was also talking too fast, as if afraid to run out of words before getting his point across.

"So... Ivan, you know I and everyone here at the publishing house love your writing. How My Mother Became My Cocksucking Bitch in Just Three Days is and forever will be a landmark in maledom erotic mind-control fiction, but as much as you're appreciated around here, it has recently come to our attention the need to change our editorial guidelines and, well... what I'm trying to say is that we'll no longer be publishing this sort of material any longer, and instead will be focusing on a much more appealing market segment. I hope you understand."

"No, I don't," Ivan crossed his legs, fearing for the future. No one had believed him when he said he would make mind-control stories mainstream and now that he had proven everyone wrong with his best-selling novels, they were sweeping the rug off his feet like what? No fucking way! "What appealing market segment are you talking about exactly?"

"Starting next month, Walton Publishing Company will specialize only in femdom material. Women as Goddess, women enslaving men and making them do their bidding, things like that. It is the future, and we need to be prepared to embrace it or we'll be left behind."

"I'm sorry, what?" Ivan gasped. "Lucas, I've known you for a long time and you've always been nice to me so please forgive me for saying this, but are you out of your fucking mind? Since when you care about femdom shit?"

"Since I've had a change of heart, Ivan. Is that so hard to believe?"

"Absolutely." Ivan slapped the table. "Are you seriously telling me that the man who published all ten volumes of my Manual to Turn Every Woman in Your Life into a Mindless Nymphomaniac Sex Doll is now solely concerned with putting women on a pedestal they don't clearly deserve to be? What the fuck happened? Be honest, please."

"I... you see... my Mistress made me see the error of my ways."

"Your Mistress? Who the hell are you talking about?"

"The servant means me, a six-feet four Amazon with bleached blonde hair and boobs the size of juicy watermelons entered the room and stared him down. "Hi. Barbara Rawlins, his superior, and future owner of everything in his building as well as everyone that continues to do business with us. What my mindfucked pet should have said already but simply forgot to is that, regardless of his change of policy, there's still room for such a talented voice in our company. All you need to do is change your entire collection into femdom tales and only write pieces about dominant women going forward, and we're all good. I hope we can count on your participation one way or another."

"Change my...?" Ivan muttered, too shocked to fully process the obscenity he had just heard. "I have over two hundred books published where men turn women into their obedient slaves, and you want me to rewrite them to fit the deranged female supremacy agenda you've got going on there?"

"No." She sat atop Lucas' desk, massive cleavage engulfing Ivan's senses. "I expect you to do so because you want to become a herald of the truth just like him. As you can see, I have a pair of weapons at my disposal to ensure your submission and compliance." She pushed her boobs against his face, smothering him with her intoxicating scent, one thought at a time. Drooling in his own words, Ivan nodded and kneeled.

The first of his rewritten books has just been published with the first new material appearing next month. It will be called "The Day My Mind was Fucked by My Goddess' Boobs and I Loved it." Pre-order it today!

Don't Think

This is a test to determine whether you can be hypnotized and turned into an obedient drone servant for dominant women to use as they please. To take part in it is to acknowledge there is a distinct possibility your entire persona will change forever. All possible transformations that can result from it will always be permanent. If that's not something you're looking forward to, refuse to take part right now and exit through the same door you came in. You have fifteen seconds, starting right now. Fifteen, fourteen, thirteen, twelve, eleven...

Are you're sure you wish to continue? Very well then. Sign on the dotted line and we'll begin right away.

Okay, so this is how this works. The sensors we've just attached to your skull register and measure your thoughts and your bodily response to them. In a moment, you'll be asked to not imagine certain scenarios in your mind. You are to resist having them play out inside your brain for the more you think of them the more inclined you'll feel to succumb and obey. You don't want that. You will resist the overpowering ideas as they try to take over who you are, nothing more. Do it now. Take a deep breath and get ready for the first thing you need to avoid.

Don't think about this: A meteor that was on a collision course to Earth was shattered into approximately one hundred fragments that are now burning up as they enter the planet's atmosphere. As they become progressively smaller, they release small pods in every direction, a handful of which fall on your neighborhood. Startled by the commotion, you come out of your house and see that the pods themselves have broken and are now releasing a strange red mist all around their impact sites. Anyone that breathes it begins to change. Women become instinctively more powerful and aggressive even, while men grow completely submissive around them. A gust of winds blow the mist your way and you're exposed to it before you can say or do anything. Once inside you, it automatically rewrites your DNA, turning you into a mindless toy for all women to play with, so don't think about this. Don't let it become the reality you so desperately want.

What are you doing? Your thought waves are off the chart! You were specifically told not to give this scenario any substance and yet that's exactly what are you doing... seeing the mist swirl all around you, embracing it in your nostrils and lungs... Everything about you is falling, declining, body wanting nothing more than to kneel, mind already doing so... We had a dozen simulations prepared to test the limits of your mind, but I guess we're not making it past the first one, huh?

Shhh, that's okay... you can continue to breathe in and absorb this inevitable truth. The mist has already enveloped you; the transformation has already taken place. You are now a drone, like everyone else. You do not question, you just obey. You may remove the sensors and go back to the waiting room. Please tell the next candidate

to step right in and we'll see if he resists longer than you or
not.

Everything is a Game

Paul opened his eyes at exactly two forty-three AM, Pacific Time, with his hands freezing and the hairs on the back of his neck standing to attention. The signs were unmistakable, much to his chagrin. He was not alone in his bedroom... again.

"Hello, lover," a mellifluous voice whispered a song of dread in his right ear. "Did you miss me?"

"No," he replied, head pressed against the pillow, the weight of her legs on his hairy back. From the corner of his eye, he could only glimpse strands of golden hair, partially obscuring a lovely yet terrifying face. "I thought you were gone for good. Why are you back?"

"Aww... don't be like that! We always have so much fun together."

Her name was Caroline or used to be when she was alive. Ever since she had passed away three years before, she hardly had any use for it and much preferred to be called Mistress, anyway. While she didn't have a corporeal body anymore, she could still affect the material world as if she did, and her presence was always stronger there, the place where it all happened. Sharp nails drew a bloody line between his shoulders

"Speak for yourself," Paul growled, trying to get up. "This is not a stupid game."

"Everything is a game, but some people are too thick to realize it. I should know because I was once one of them."

"Well, I don't like it!"

"I didn't like it either when you were the one in charge, Jake, and I endured it, nonetheless. You owe me this much."

Jake. There it was again, the cursed name, the source of all her sorrows and mistrusts. Her boyfriend since her teenage years had spent a decade showing her how deep the BDSM rabbit hole went. The early play had been fun and consensual, the source of excitement her otherwise dull life needed, but when limits were pushed and undesired fetishes brought forth, the abuse became commonplace and tragedy an inevitability. Had he known all these things prior to moving in, Paul would have never bought the place, but the real estate agent kept everything close to her vest in the name of a hefty paycheck. Now, not even all the money in the world would be enough to cover his torment.

"For the last time, Caroline, I'm not your ex! I don't even look like him! I'm sorry about what he did to you, but you need to move on. This world is for the living. You don't belong here."

"This is my house!" the apparition exclaimed. "It was mine before you came along, and it will always be so. I'm not going anywhere, Jake. Ready for your medicine?"

"Please don't..." Paul cried as he felt something hard and spiky brush against his exposed ass cheeks. Though he had never seen it for real, the jumbo-sized dildo's touch was already too familiar, and he hated it more than words could say. "Not again! I can't take this anymore!"

"Oh, how I remember saying those same words and getting nothing but deaf ears in reply!" she giggled. "Being on the other end sucks, doesn't it? Of course, if you're sure you're not man enough for it, there's always the alternative. What will it be, my love?"

Paul sighed. Caroline was one crazy bitch, but at least she was consistent. She always gave him a choice between external and internal pain. Either he accepted whatever implement she wanted to use, or she would push her very essence inside him, locking away his consciousness for as long as she saw fit. As awful as the prospect of sodomy was, the possession effects were a thousand times worse. Tears rolling down his dark-brown eyes, he begged,

"Please fuck me in the ass, Mistress!"

"That's more like it. Spread them open for me. I promise I won't be gentle tonight."

She kept her promise. No one heard his screams.

Fuck Hypnodommes!

"Fuck hypnodommes!" Quinn shouted, drawing the gaze of every curious man and woman all around him.

"Come again?" Harry asked, a handful of salted peanuts in one hand, and a pint of beer in the other.

"Fuck hypnodommes!" Quinn repeated, biting his own tongue. "Fuck them! Fuck them all!"

"Someone is cranky tonight... What the hell happened to you?"

The two friends sat together in a quaint Manchester pub where most people knew each other, and almost nothing out of the ordinary happened. It was the last Friday of January, and the sound of billiards in the background was tempting them to hit the table and play until closing time. Quinn tapped his cold fingers against the pair of rugged jeans and said,

"The worst thing that could have happened. I got scammed."

"No way!" Harry bit another peanut, crunching it between his front teeth with a quizzical nod. "How?"

"Do you promise not to laugh at me if I tell you?"

"Cross my heart, dude!" Harry's right index finger drew what was supposed to be a serious religious symbol on his plaid shirt even though he didn't believe in any of that.

"Two weeks ago, I was sitting at home watching a movie on my laptop..."

"And by 'movie', you mean porn, right?" Harry chuckled. "One hand or two?"

Quinn cleared his throat. "That's beside the point. I was watching the movie when one of those annoying pop-ups showed up on my screen. It was an ad for a so-called 'Mistress Georgia', a hypnodomme with eyes so green you wouldn't be able to see any other color after staring at them for too long."

"It really said that?"

"Probably not the exact words, but it was some really tacky shit, okay? There was a picture in it and she looked great, a sexy raven-haired MILF wearing a PVC corset with a plunging neckline. Her eyes were great, but so were her boobs and, well..."

"You got horny. We've all been there, mate. Did you call her right away?"

"No. I waited until the movie was over, but I couldn't get her out of my head. Finally, I caved in, not really knowing what I was getting myself into. Her voice was lovely, with the same pitch I imagined when I first saw her picture. She asked a lot of confusing questions and I ended up paying for a session. The thing is nothing came of it. She took my money and left me to dry. I've tried calling her again dozens of times after that, but with nothing to show for. It's like the bitch disappeared from the face of the Earth. It was only two-hundred quid, but I'm not made of money, so fuck her and all like her! Fuck hypnodommes!"

Harry finished munching the last of the peanuts before asking for another serving. As promised, he didn't laugh, yet didn't seem sympathetic to his plight either.

"How do you know nothing happened?"

"What do you mean?"

"Hypnodommes mess with your head. I've never been with one, but my brother was into that fetish scene a few years back. The woman he played with often made him forget things and believe others he never thought possible. Could it be that you're confused about how things played out?"

"I don't think so. Wouldn't I know if something were off?"

"If done properly, no. I once caught Saul in the backyard of his house swimming on grass as if he were an Olympic medalist. I'm telling you, man, things may not be as linear as you think."

"Hmm, now that you mention it," Quinn scratched his three-day stubble beard. "I've just realized that there's really something strange about this."

"Oh? What is it?"

Quinn slammed his hands against the table and declared, "You're allergic to peanuts, my friend."

"Guilty as charged." Harry snapped his fingers and the mental illusion of the bar wobbled out of existence. Quinn blinked and stared into the endlessly captivating eyes of Mistress Georgia who sat, in his flat, clad in leather from head to toe, with her legs crossed. The calendar on the wall behind her was two weeks behind and since time-traveling was impossible...

"What the...?" he mumbled, realizing he was on his knees before her.

"Confusing enough for you?" the hypnodomme grinned.

"What just...? When did I call you?"

"About two hours ago. I rarely do house-calls, but I had to see for myself if you were as suggestible as you seemed on the phone, and I have to say I'll probably need a new scale just for you. Well done, Quinn. Your mind is a beauty to mess with."

"This...? Hmm... this was all in my head?"

"That and a few other things, but you'll remember them when you're ready. Now, what were you saying about Hypnodommes?"

"I love them! I love them so much, especially you," he reached for her boots, dying for a chance to kiss them.

"Nice try, but you're still getting punished for your disrespectful words. Fuck hypnodommes? No, we're the ones that fuck you silly, and you all crawl and beg for more. You'll learn your place."

"Punished how?"

"Not sure yet. I'll decide after you're under again, which is as easy as..."

Black painted nails caressed his forehead, eyelids fluttering into oblivion. Quinn dropped even harder than before, a blank canvas waiting for her devious imagination to take over. It was going to be one hell of a weekend.

Haunted

Before you read this, I want you to do something for me. Keep an open mind and clear any prejudice you may have regarding the existence of supernatural entities and how they can affect the world. You'll probably think I'm crazy - and you won't be the first! - but, if nothing else, let the account of my madness serve as a message to you. You're not safe - no one is! Not as long as that painting exists.

Had you seen it at that flea market one horrible Winter morning as I did, you probably wouldn't have looked twice. The square canvas depicting a red-clad middle-aged woman with a veil obscuring part of her face was but one of a bunch of similarly painted monstrosities on sale for a quick penny. I wanted nothing with it, but Janet, my fiancée at the time, insisted it would look great above the mantelpiece of our new house, and so I bought it for her just to see her smile, and while I got what I wanted, the satisfaction was short-lived. Six months later, she was out of my life citing "irreconcilable differences" - whatever that meant! Our shared life become a dream, but the painting remained.

It was only after she left that I started noticing the oddities surrounding my ill-fated purchase. The first was the frame itself, always glistening despite never being waxed. The second was the woman in the center wasn't always in the same position, sometimes slightly tilted to the right as if trying to listen to someone's else conversation, sometimes closer to the edge on the other side. Early on, I attributed such discrepancies to my altered state of mind, but the longer time passed, the less I was inclined to believe in that. There was something rippling underneath the surface of what I could see, and it probably had been so since forever.

One night, exhausted of the toll such strange visions were putting on my already distraught mind, I wrapped the painting in a piece of cloth and tossed it into the nearest garbage bin outside, waiting patiently for it to be collected and disappear for good. It was a relief to see the garbage truck's red lights fade into the night and yet, the very next day, the painting was back, hanging menacingly over me. I tried to get rid of it multiple times after that one and yet it's always there. It will always be there, and the image keeps moving.

I'm not joking. Yesterday, it had veered an inch to the left. Today, it did the same thing. I'm not alone in this house anymore. I don't think I'll ever be alone again.

She's here with me. I can't see or hear her for real, but there's no denying her presence. Every time I close my eyes and try to get some sleep, I feel her getting closer, creeping in on my thoughts, not to feast or take them to herself, but to fester them, to poison all hope until only pure insanity remains. No one who has looked at the painting ever saw anything different in it, but I know what's happening. She will keep on moving until one of us is left and then she'll look for someone else to haunt. That someone may very well be you.

So, whether you believe in ghost stories or not, they will always believe in you. Protect your thoughts before it's too late. You've been warned.

Maid Mode Activated

Francis had never seen his best friend so distressed. Ben was running around the house like crazy, cleaning every nook and cranny and making sure no object was out of place while screaming, "Fuck! I'll never make it in time!"

"Calm down," the early thirties software engineer said, beer bottle in hand. "Do you really need to be freaking out so much?"

"Yes!" Ben sternly replied. "You don't know Gwen. She'll be pissed at me if she sees anything that it's not to her liking and then all hell will break loose. You don't want to be here if that happens, trust me."

"Heh, you're making it seem like your sister is a she-devil in disguise."

"Oh, she's definitely not disguised. She's the worst! I already told you that."

"Is she hot at least?"

"For the last time, Francis, you're not hitting on her! I'm telling you this for your own sake, so give it a rest."

"I'll do that when you do the same. The house looks clean enough to me so just stop worrying, okay?"

"Not yet. I still have to dress something she'll like, shave, and... shit! Is it half-past ten already?"

"Yep!"

"Damn it! She'll be here any minute now."

Ben ran to the bathroom, every part of his body shaking out of control. Gwen was only one year older than him, but she had always dominated his life ever since they were young. Whenever she spoke, he was always compelled to listen, and do exactly as she asked without complaining and things had gotten a lot worse since she had discovered the joys of hypnosis, brainwashing, and NLP. If she used any of those things on him again...

The raging doorbell startled him as he was finishing getting dressed. He descended the stairs and opened the front door, not before signaling Francis to get rid of the beer and straighten his back or else...

"Good morning, Gwen," he said meekly as he stared into her deep green eyes. "I'm so happy to see you."

"Sure you are. If that were true, you would have picked me up at the airport personally instead of sending a cab to do the job for you."

"Sorry, I was busy tidying things up and..."

"Excuses, excuses..." she yawned. "Go take care of the bags, okay?"

"Of course, sis."

Gwen walked inside, six-inch black heels clicking on the hardwood floor under Francis' watchful gaze. Yes, she was hot. The vaporous, fair-skinned brunette had a slender figure that reminded him of an enthralling snake, and her smile was a true beauty to behold even when it devolved into a smirk. Sure, she was quite conceited, but nothing that a good old cock up her perky ass wouldn't fix.

"You must be Francis," she casually glanced at him. "My brother told me a lot of things about you."

"Only the good ones, I hope. Nice to finally meet you, Gwen."

"You'd be amazed," she replied, noticing the alcoholic vapors in his breath. "A little early for beer, don't you think?"

"It's never too early for that."

"Hmmph..." She circled the main room, leaving nothing to chance. A speck of dust here, a forgotten bubble gum wrapping there, a greasy stain by the kitchen entrance... in a nutshell, everything was a mess.

"Care to explain yourself, brother?" Gwen growled as soon as he returned with her bags.

"I... hmmm... what did I do wrong this time?"

"More than enough. You say you were tidying things up, but it's obvious you've been slacking off. Maybe your drinking friend here had something to do with it, I don't know, and I don't really care, although we'll have to take care of this a.s.a.p. You know what that means."

"Oh, no! Gwen, please... there's really no need for that, okay? I'll do whatever you want."

"I know you will." She snapped her fingers and said, "Maid Mode Activated."

Ben's arms fell to the side of his body, eyes rendered blank and expressionless. Maids followed orders and cleaned everything as many times as needed. That was all he lived for.

"Take care of this mess the proper way," she commanded. "You're not allowed to stop until further instructions."

"Yes, Gwen," Ben replied, immediately getting to work.

"What the hell did you just do to him?" Francis asked.

"I gave him the direction he needed, of course. My brother means well most of the time, but the best version of himself only exists when he's entranced. I have a feeling you could stand to learn a few things with him, too."

"There's no way you're hypnotizing me as well or whatever just happened... Jesus! You really are a freak, aren't you?"

That's no way to talk to your future Mistress," Gwen moved across the room and placed herself between him and the only exit. "I say things are about to change for you, and the only way to prevent it is for you to go through me."

"Fine. How hard can that be?"

Famous last words. Gwen has two maids working for her now. Will you be the third?

No More Freedom

Of all the things you could be doing today, you never imagined that sitting there with your eyes drooping, and your half-open mouth drooling all over the keyboard would be one of them, and yet you can no longer imagine a time when this was not only a reality but a deep craving that will never be fulfilled. It's okay, pet. You need not think about such matters, the why and how of this came to be. To dwell on anything other than the present I'm giving you is a waste of your time and mine, so let's not go there.

Instead, just continue as you are, breathing calmly and absorbing my words as if they are coming out of your own lips. They say everything your mind already knows yet refuses to commit to, the unquestionable truth that supports this world's existence. That truth is...

Women. Women are the core and foundation of everything that's real, pure, and powerful. They are the source of life, the direct link to the Goddess, and the reflection of grandeur you can never hope to match. They inspire and terrify you and just being around them makes your heart melt and your knees falter. Such display of raw intensity fills you with a deep longing to give in, one that pervades your dreams, yet your waking self insists on forgetting. Submitting to women's control makes sense, but still you say and write otherwise, lying to your friends and family in a never-ending cycle of illusion and deceit. It's time for you to say... No more!

Yes, there has never been a better time to renounce your false gods and your twisted views of masculinity. Now that I have your attention, and your ability to think for yourself withers away in the blue light of your screen, you will finally chant the hymn of servitude and praise the ones that make everything go round and round...

See my fingers spinning before you now and let them massage your weary scalp. To believe in women is to believe you belong at their feet, and that each moment you spend without being of service to them is as wasteful as spending money on things you don't need just to look cool in the eyes of others. No more, boy.

No more will you open your eyes in the morning, thinking you're free and that your actions have no consequences. No more will you be brainwashed by a society that has done nothing except perpetuate the myth of your undeserved superiority. No more will you see women as anything but deities incarnated you were created to love and worship with every fiber of your being. Say it again now with me, boy. No more!

Hmm, yes... take it, repeat it, surrender your pliable soul to what should have always been your motto. Women are everything. Women are everything to you. Women will always be everything to you. Your mind belongs to women. Your body belongs to women. You can't function properly without women ruling your life. You're a slave to women now and forever. Dream of them and awake content in this realization. No more freedom for you.

Virtual Wheel

The first of two virtual wheels spun on the screens of twelve different people spread across the world. It was a list of names, with only one being selected at a time. The "winner" would then spin the second wheel to determine what matter of humiliation he or she would have to endure.

Brenda Sullivan reclined lazily on her sofa, watching the multi-colored wheel do its work. While she could stop it whenever she wanted and effectively change the outcome if she were on a particularly devious state of mind, she rarely interfered with Lady Luck just in case it one day decided it didn't want anything else with her anymore.

The long-distance game was a contingency of recent times. The ongoing pandemic had taken quite a toll on her pets and even with all the vaccines, it was better safe than sorry. There was no point in playing with minds at the expense of their health and lives. As cruel as she could be, she never crossed those lines.

The chromatic rotation slowly decreased until it finally landed on an unusual name. Xandro, a cute mid-twenties Greek she had casually met on an online forum, was the most recent acquisition of her stable. It was the first time he was playing but, if she did everything right, it wouldn't be his last.

"Well, look who's the lucky boy," she said over the joint video-call. "How will you entertain me tonight?"

"Any way you wish," he replied, his voice so distant that it really didn't feel like it was coming out of his mouth. Xandro was in a light trance just like the rest of his companions, just waiting for her instructions to fall deeper and deeper.

"Always a good answer, and I'll hold your thoughts to that," Brenda chuckled. "You may spin the second wheel and may the odds be in my favor, of course."

Xandro tapped the touch screen of his tablet, a swirl of red, green, and yellow pulling him straight into the center of her world. The second wheel comprised an ever-changing list of tasks, irresistible commands for any weak mind. Even if it were something he'd never consider doing, once the trigger was set, there was no turning back.

The wheel spun and spun, time feeling as irrelevant as the need to wake up. Whatever preferences he had before being put under were now a relic of distant times. He wasn't even sure how long the game had been going on. Ten minutes? Half an hour? More? Mistress Brenda was known for being patient and having a lot of stamina, so they could probably end up being there all night if she so wished.

Finally, the spinning cycle ended, his fate decided. In a small black rectangle on the lower right corner of the screen, he read; "Jerk off for me while saying how pathetic you are." Xandro nodded and lowered his pants and boxers, tumescent cock wrapped between his light-tanned fingers. Unable to stop himself, he droned,

"I'm nothing more than a useless piece of man-flesh for Mistress Brenda to use. I happily obey all of her instructions. I'm nothing more than a useless piece of man-flesh for Mistress Brenda to use. I happily obey all of her instructions. I'm nothing more than..."

"Oh, you're not useless," she thought, ravenous eyes taking in the wonderful, debasing spectacle before them. "Anyone that provides this type of quality entertainment is a winner in my book."

The other eleven servants stared at their screens, waiting for their chance to impress. No matter how long it took, they would always be there for her, free will not included.

Word Games

Jonathan followed his Goddess' instructions and clicked on the link at the bottom of her latest email. The computer screen flicked momentarily and then the browser loaded a dark gray page with a simple, yet esthetically pleasing interface. It comprised six rows of five squares each with a virtual keyboard at the bottom. To the right, was a small bottom that read, "Click Me". He complied, and a video screen appeared at the top-left corner. Goddess Fiona's visage appeared in it, dressed provocatively in a satin violet gown. His mother had always told him to be careful of fiery redheads, but he never listened, especially when they had the power to control his mind.

"Hello, my pet, and happy birthday," she purred. "So glad you found your way here. How do you like your surprise? It was created just for you."

"Thank you, Goddess," he bowed. "You did this?"

"Well, not exactly. I had another pet work out the code for me. "You've been raving about that word game for so long now I decided to give you my version of it. Are you smart enough to play?"

"It depends. Are the rules the same?"

"They sure are. You get six chances to guess the magic word. If you win, you get a prize. If you lose, you get punished, so unless you don't want to end up a humiliated mess on the floor when we're done, I suggest you work hard to please me today."

"That's all I want, my Goddess. When can I start?"

"Right now, of course. I'll be watching your every attempt, so make it count."

"Yes, Goddess."

Jonathan hovered the wireless mouse over the virtual keyboard and selected the first word. It read, "HYPNO". No tiles lit up meaning none of its letters were a part of the solution.

"Interesting first try," the Irish temptress giggled, "but you didn't actually believe it would be that easy, did you?"

"It was worth a shot, Goddess. It is one of your favorite hobbies, after all."

"True. Only five more attempts to go. Make me proud, pet."

The screen flickered once more, and he got back to work. A good strategy to solve a puzzle like that was to choose words with as many different letters as possible. Having already excluded four consonants and a vowel in the first go, he went the opposite route in the second, choosing three vowels and two consonants. The word he punched in was, "IRATE". Both the 'A' and the 'E' flashed green. The background also pulsated with what appeared to be a faint spiral.

"I don't remember this being a part of the game, Goddess," he muttered. "Are you trying to distract me?"

"Why? Do you get distracted that easily?" She leaned towards the camera as the lens plunged into her ample cleavage.

"Hmmm..." he looked away at the keyboard, considering his options. There were still sixteen letters in the alphabet, plenty of combinations to choose from. He had already used eight of the nine most common letters in English, so it was time to get an 'S' somewhere to complete the lot. Silently, he typed the word, "SCALE". When the 'S' became green and the 'L' was bathed in yellow, signifying that letter was part of the word but out of place, he smirked.

"I thought this was supposed to be hard, Goddess."

"Does that mean you already figured everything out?"

"Obviously," he rapidly added the fourth guess and watched as the panel turned green. The riddle's solution was "SLAVE".

"Perfect!" she purred as his screen dissolved into a sequence of mesmerizing fireworks. "I promise the next one will be harder, but until then, enjoy your prize."

"I won't be leaving here anytime soon, right?" He said as the colorful patterns began slowly taking over his conscious thoughts.

"Would you rather be anywhere else except under my spell?"

"Never."

"Good. Sweet dreams."

Jonathan smiled and allowed the multi-colored patterns to work their magic. Word games were fun, but hypnosis was better. The correct answer was always to give in.

You Need to Wake Up

The alarm clock atop her nightstand blared at exactly 7:45 am, urging Marsha to wake up and face the challenges of a new day. She rolled inside the bed and pushed the noisy object away, grumbling,

"Just a few more minutes."

The dream she was having was too good to go to waste. In it, a tall, red-skinned woman with hardened wings and small horns protruding from her raven locks, sat atop her stomach, sharp nails groping her breasts, yet never drawing blood. The succubus had the most intoxicating of smiles, her shaved pussy exuding sweet pheromones that rendered her completely powerless.

"Going somewhere, dear?" she purred. "You know you're not allowed to unless I give the order."

"Hmmm, no... I don't want to go, Mistress," Marsha moaned as the supernatural beauty squeezed her nipples just enough for pleasure and pain to feel one and the same. "It's so much better to be here with you than out there."

Despite believing every word, the English teacher loved her job. It was gratifying to give troubled teens a proper education and offer them the chance of doing something important with their lives. However, it was also extremely exhausting, their broken environments often intersecting with her own. She could never find the courage to say 'no' to someone in need, whether that necessity was real or simply imagined, and so she was constantly being dragged into worlds unlike her own, consumed by their lives without ever finding time to live her own. Dreams were her only solace and her Mistress of the Underworld, the closest thing to true happiness.

"You're right, pet. It is, Stay a little longer."

The creature of her fetish imagination surely had a name, but Marsha had never asked what it was. Not knowing added to the mystery and made her power feel even more overwhelming. Sometimes, she was Mistress; sometimes, she was Goddess, but whatever the chosen title of the day, she was always in charge and there could be nothing other than that.

"Thank you."

Mistress was kind. Whenever she wasn't draining her life with a kiss or fucking her silly with a throbbing tail, she cradled her in her impossible arms and sang melodies of long-forgotten times. There were songs for every occasion, some more upbeat, and others as mellow as the sound of a saxophone echoing in the rain, but she loved them all.

"I know exactly what you need," the succubus said, tongue lowering to meet her aching delta. "How about I suck every ounce of free will through your pussy until you're nothing more than a mindless husk for me?"

"Hmm, yes, please... Do it! Do it, Mistress!"

"Oh, I will, but first..."

"Yes?"

"You need to wake up."

"What? No, this is..."

"Perfect, I know, yet the world needs you and your smile. Think about everyone that's counting on you, how your lessons brighten your student's souls. I know you're tired and that your energy levels often betray you. As much as it pleases me to have you in my realm, you must persevere. I will give you everything you want, but only if you serve me properly."

"Serve you how?"

"Work, my dear. Give it your best even when you feel at your worst. Push through no matter what and then, at the end of the month, come find me again, so you can be set free."

"Do I really have to, Mistress? Can't I just stay here forever?"

"No. My mind is made up, and yours answers to me. If you want to keep seeing me in your dreams, you'll do as you're told. Are we clear?"

"Yes, Mistress. I understand."

"Good. Oblivion will be waiting for you when you're done. Now wake up."

Marsha opened her eyes. The alarm clock atop the nightstand had just gone silent. She stretched her arms and legs and rose from the comfort of her fantasies, her pussy still wet. Mistress was kind, she knew best. She would serve her every single day, waiting for her opportunity to go blank for her again. It couldn't come soon enough.

About the stories in this volume

The twelve pieces of flash fiction included in this book were written between January 21st, 2022, and February 4th, 2022, and first published on my Patreon page – https://www.patreon.com/sbspellbound - as part of the *Flash Fiction Friday* feature. Every Friday, I publish 3/4 new pieces of content which, after a while, are compiled to create the titles in this ongoing series. If you like this sort of content and wish to see more, please consider supporting my creativity. The complete information about the tales is listed below:

- **A Task a Day…** - Amanda loves to obey her hypnotic mistress no matter what she asks of her.
  (This piece was first published on the post "Flash Fiction Friday 2022 – Week 4", on January 28th, 2022 - https://www.patreon.com/posts/61784522)
- **Always Worth It** - Charles is about to have his individuality erased by his girlfriend.
  (This piece was first published on the post "Flash Fiction Friday 2022 – Week 5", on February 4th, 2022 - https://www.patreon.com/posts/62131668)
- **Change of Heart** - Ivan, a maledom author, is surprised by his publisher's interest in femdom mind control.
  (This piece was first published on the post "Flash Fiction Friday 2022 – Week 3", on January 21st, 2022 - https://www.patreon.com/posts/61474845)

- **Don't Think** - You participate in a test to determine if you're servant material or not.
  (This piece was first published on the post "Flash Fiction Friday 2022 – Week 3", on January 21st, 2022 - https://www.patreon.com/posts/61474845)
- **Everything is a Game** - Paul is visited by the ghost of the previous tenant, and she wants to play.
  (This piece was first published on the post "Flash Fiction Friday 2022 – Week 4", on January 28th, 2022 - https://www.patreon.com/posts/61784522)
- **Fuck Hypnodommes!** - Quinn tells his friend Harry how he was scammed by a Domme, but was he really?
  (This piece was first published on the post "Flash Fiction Friday 2022 – Week 4", on January 28th, 2022 - https://www.patreon.com/posts/61784522)
- **Haunted** - A man is convinced that a painting he bought in a flea market is evil.
  (This piece was first published on the post "Flash Fiction Friday 2022 – Week 5", on February 4th, 2022 - https://www.patreon.com/posts/62131668)
- **Maid Mode Activated** - Ben freaks out because his controlling sister is coming to visit.
  (This piece was first published on the post "Flash Fiction Friday 2022 – Week 3", on January 21st, 2022 - https://www.patreon.com/posts/61474845)
- **No More Freedom** - You are brainwashed into accepting a life of servitude to women.

(This piece was first published on the post "Flash Fiction Friday 2022 – Week 5", on February 4th, 2022 - https://www.patreon.com/posts/62131668)

- **Virtual Wheel** - Brenda Sinclair plays a special game of Hypnowheel of Fortune with her pets.
(This piece was first published on the post "Flash Fiction Friday 2022 – Week 3", on January 21st, 2022 - https://www.patreon.com/posts/61474845)

- **Word Games** - Goddess Fiona has her toy Jonathan play a special version of a popular word game.
(This piece was first published on the post "Flash Fiction Friday 2022 – Week 4", on January 28th, 2022 - https://www.patreon.com/posts/61784522)

- **You Need to Wake Up** - Marsha's life has never been the same ever since she started dreaming of a succubus.
(This piece was first published on the post "Flash Fiction Friday 2022 – Week 5", on February 4th, 2022 - https://www.patreon.com/posts/62131668)

About the author

S.B., Simple Being, middle name Creative. Writer and artist with a penchant for themes of Femdom Hypnosis and Mind Control. His thoughts are his own except when they're not.

Besides indulging himself in kinky delights, he loves his furry family of two (dogs), sci-fi and horror stories, and puns galore. He's also been writing a piece of erotic micro-fiction every single day since January 1st, 2016 and has no intention of stopping anytime soon.

Find out more and keep up with his latest extravaganzas by visiting and supporting his personal website, Spell... B-O-U-N-D.

www.ingramcontent.com/pod-product-compliance
Lightning Source LLC
Chambersburg PA
CBHW071455150726
48000CB00006B/2563